P9-CFJ-612

Puddle Jumpers

Written by
Anne Margaret Lewis

Illustrated by Nancy Cote

Sky Pony Press
New York

Sky Pony Press books may be purchased in bulk at special discounts for sales promotion, corporate gifts, fund-raising, or educational purposes. Special editions can also be created to specifications. For details, contact the Special Sales Department, Sky Pony Press, 307 West 36th Street, 11th Floor, New York, NY 10018 or info@skyhorsepublishing.com.

Sky Pony® is a registered trademark of Skyhorse Publishing, Inc.®, a Delaware corporation.

Visit our website at www.skyponypress.com.

10 9 8 7 6 5 4 3 2 1

Manufactured in China, September 2015
This product conforms to CPSIA 2008

Library of Congress Cataloging-in-Publication Data is available on file.

Cover design by Gretchen Schuler
Cover illustration credit Nancy Cote

Print ISBN: 978-1-63450-185-9
Ebook ISBN: 978-1-63450-933-6

On a spring-filled day in the month of May
the rain poured down in a stream.
A rainbow appeared with a gleam and a glow,
and a puddle awaited Sam's dream.

Mother said, "No! No jumping in puddles!
You must keep clean today!"

But Sam dipped his galoshes, with a *splish* and a *splash*,
when the puddle invited him to play.

The puddle whispered, "Jump, Puddle Jumper, jump!"
As Sam jumped, he wished . . .

I wish I were a frog in a pond
with a hat and some spots and a magical wand.

Leap, Puddle Jumper, leap!

I wish I were a croc in the glades
with pink polka dots and teeth like blades.

Snap, Puddle Jumper, snap!

I wish I were a penguin in the south,
wearing a tux with my beak-honking mouth.

Honk, Puddle Jumper, honk!

I wish I were a brave bold shark
with a sword and sharp teeth in an ocean park.

Chomp, Puddle Jumper, chomp!

I wish I were a red-striped flamingo,
prancing and dancing the one-legged tango.

Dance, Puddle Jumper, dance!

I wish I were a purple polar bear,
plunging through the Arctic with my purple polar hair.

Plunge, Puddle Jumper, plunge!

I wish I were a toucan in a tree,
swinging in the rainforest, drinking iced tea.

Swing, Puddle Jumper, swing!

I wish I were a swift dragonfly,
flying above the marsh like a top secret spy.

Fly, Puddle Jumper, fly!

I wish I were floating in a yellow submarine,
singing ocean songs, playing my tambourine.

Sing, Puddle Jumper, sing!

I wish I were a scuba diver in the Lavender Sea, blowing silly bubbles with a silly manatee.

Blow, Puddle Jumper, blow!

I wish I were a snail in a race.
I'd scurry in the sand, winning first place.

I wish I were a fish in a stream
with bluish-green stripes, eating chocolate ice cream.

Sam stopped for a moment.
The puddle whispered again.

"Jump, Puddle Jumper, jump!"

As Sam jumped he wished, and the most magical thing happened...

Mom saw Sam smile and with a *leap*
then a *thwump*, she jumped, too, cheering,
"Jump, Puddle Jumper, jump!"